LYNN'S CHOICE

JANET KELLY

ISBN: 978-1-7354029-0-1 (paperback)
ISBN: 978-1-7354029-2-5 (hardcover)
ISBN: 978-1-7354029-1-8 (ebook)

*To my Mom Imogene, who first suggested I
write for Young Adults, I Love and
Miss you, thank you.*

*To my kids Heather, Janalee and Michael.
For their encouragement and believing
in me. I love you all.*

*To Doug my love for his constant support
and having my back.*

CONTENTS

INTRODUCTION

Lynn a teenage high school student trapped in a vicious cycle of drugs. Being pulled in two very different directions by her friends. You will be captivated by her experiences and her fighting spirit.

CHAPTER

1

Lynn could smell the rich aroma of freshly cut grass. She was reminded of when she was small. She had watched as her Dad mowed the lawn, thinking him so big and strong and loving him so much. She sat wondering what had happened to the man who used to give her rides on his back and would take her for ice cream on hot summer days. The man who held her and told her he would always be with her seemed to have disappeared since the death of her Mom.

Three years had gone by, and it had been hard on them both. So unexpected. Her mom had gone out for a quick trip to the store when a truck from out of nowhere ran a red light, smashing into her car and killing her instantly. One minute she had a mom, the next she didn't. Lynn didn't even get to say good-bye.

There were so many things she had wanted to say to and do with her mom that now she couldn't do. Sometimes she felt cheated and angry. Her dad didn't seem to realize how hard the pain and loss had been on her. The more she needed him, the more he pulled away. He started working longer hours and spending less time with her.

Lynn looked down at her watch, realizing she was late meeting Jade. She jumped up and hurried on. Lynn and Jade had been best friends since childhood, so, after three months apart, Lynn was anxious to be with her friend and catch up on all the news.

They met at Jake's, the local hamburger stand. It had ten booths, their red vinyl seats worn and tattered. In the summer you stick to the seats. In the winter they are cold. The tabletops had initials carved into them. Nobody seemed to mind any of it. The jukebox was full of their favorite songs, some of which had been replaced after being worn out from being played so often. The hamburgers and fries were greasy and the coke is syrupy, but that's how they like it.

Lynn and Jade spent a couple of hours catching up. Lynn talked about her dad and Jade told Lynn about her trip. Then Lynn started getting restless; she wanted to go home, so she could smoke a joint.

"Why don't we go back to my house?" She said. Dad's not there. We'll have it all to ourselves."

"Ok, maybe we can go swimming for a while too."

"Yeah we can do that. Let's go."

As they were leaving, a girl with long black wavy hair walked in. She was wearing a baby blue tank top and tight jeans.

"That's all we need," said Jade motioning toward the girl at the door.

"What do you mean?" asked Lynn.

"That girl who just walked in, she's beautiful. Look how all the guys are watching her. She acts like she owns the place and everyone in here. The way they're drooling she probably could."

"Oh come on," Lynn said laughing. "That's Riva, she is a friend of mine."

"She's what?" Jade asked, with a look of surprise.

Lynn went over and greeted Riva. The two of them laughing and talking quietly, their heads close together so no one could hear them.

When Jade joined them, Riva turned toward her, raised one eyebrow, seemed to dismiss her, and turned back to Lynn.

"Are you coming to the party at Jesse's tonight?" Riva asked.

"Yeah, I told you I would."

"Good. Jesse is hoping you'll come."

"What party? Who's Jesse?" asked Jade, nudging Lynn.

"Oh, sorry, I forgot." Said Lynn, turning to Jade. "This is Riva, Riva this is Jade."

Lynn was telling Jade about the get together and Jesse when she noticed hurt in Jade's eyes. She felt bad about forgetting to introduce Jade to Riva, so she invited her to the party.

Lynn sighed to herself with relief when

Jade declined. She knew that if Jade went, she would be uncomfortable.

On their way back to Lynn's, Jade asked where she had met Riva and how they'd become friends. Lynn told her they had met at a party, and the two of them just hit it off. What she didn't tell her was that someone had introduced her to Riva because she was selling and Lynn was buying.

"You're so different from her. It's tough to see the two of you being friends." said Jade.

"I like her, she's fun to be with, and she's a lot like you." said Lynn.

"Now that's hard to believe," said Jade shaking her head.

"You're both strong-willed, and confident."

"I don't know about that, but I do know there's something about her I don't like.

When they got to Lynn's house, Jade went swimming. Lynn went upstairs to smoke a joint that had been on her mind all day. She sat watching Jade from her bedroom window as she dove into the pool. Lynn always loved watching Jade swim. She made it seem so easy. Her slender frame looked right at home in the water, her auburn hair floating above her back as she swam. You couldn't see them, but Jade's brown eyes were sparkling, as they always did when she swam. Lynn eyed the joint in her hand and then looked back at Jade. She put it back in the draw, not wanting to get high with Jade around. The two of them swam for a couple of hours.

CHAPTER

2

Lynn assessed herself in the mirror. Her long, light blonde hair hung down her back, with strands lying over her right shoulder in front. She turned sideways, looking at her slim frame. She was wearing tight-fitting jeans and a tight-fitting t-shirt. Turning around again, she looked at her reflection and liked what she saw. "My eyes are my best feature, though," she said. She had her mom's eyes—the same shade of green and the same oval shape. She smiled to herself.

When Lynn arrived at the party, it was going strong. She could hear the music from outside. When she walked in, the smell of pot hit her hard. The smoke from cigarettes and pot was so thick that she could hardly see across the room, where Riva and Jesse sat. Riva spotted her and motioned for her to join them.

Lynn studied them from across the room. Riva's long black hair moved back and forth to the music. Her eyes were almost black, with a depth to them that Lynn could not understand. Almost like there was another life inside. She had a small nose and high cheekbones, her lips were full. Her figure slim but mature. Lynn remembered what Jade had said earlier about Riva, and had to agree that she was beautiful.

Lynn turned her attention to Jesse. His light-brown hair straight except where it lay on his collar, then it curled upward. His piercing blue eyes looked right through you. His face was oval with a firm chin. He was muscular, as if he worked out. He was a few inches taller than Lynn and Riva. Lynn liked the way he looked; she thought he was very handsome.

As Lynn approached them, Jesse handed her a joint, tightly wrapped and half gone. The sweet smell engulfed her nostrils as she took a hit. She could feel her lungs filling up with smoke, hot and smooth at the same time. With her eyes closed, she released the smoke. A wave of chills rose to the top of her head. As it slowly left her, she opened her eyes to catch sight of Jesse watching her, smiling.

"So what are you smiling about?" asked Lynn.

"You," answered Jesse.

"Why?"

"Do I need a reason?"

"I guess not,"

"How long have you and that girl you were with today been friends?' asked Riva.

"Since the third grade."

"So why didn't you bring her tonight."

"Jade doesn't get loaded, she hates drugs."

"And the two of you are friends?" asked Riva laughing. "That's kind of weird, don't you think? I mean what do you do when you're loaded, and she's not? Does she sit and watch you ?"

"No, I don't do that in front of her."

"Does she know you do?" asked Riva

"No." said Lynn annoyed.

"You're kidding".

"No I'm not. She doesn't, and I don't want her to, either. Let's talk about something else, like what's in the back room," she said, turning towards Jesse.

"Oh, you mean that white stuff,"

"Yeah, do you have any?"

"Right this way," said Jesse, motioning for her to follow him.

Lynn followed him down the hall to his room. There was a bed in one corner, a dresser, and a table on one side. Posters of rock and roll stars lined the walls. That was all that was in his room. On the table lay a mirror, and on the mirror, the white powder, coke. Six lines had been set.

Jesse gave Lynn a small plastic tube. She snorted the first line in her left nostril, the second in her right. What little was left she rubbed on her gums, then sat back on Jesse's bed and watched as Jesse and Riva took their turns. The three of them smoked another joint and then went out to join everyone.

The music turned soft from the hard, heavy sounds that had been playing, when she arrived. Lynn and Riva sat on the couch, while Jesse joined some guys in the kitchen.

"You have a crush on Jesse don't you?" asked Riva.

"Yeah he's nice. And cute."

"He likes you too."

"Maybe as a friend, but that's about it."

"Are you kidding? He hasn't taken his eyes off you since you walked in."

"Yeah right."

"That is right," said Riva as she stood up. "I think you need to start paying attention to what's going on around you, then maybe you'd see for yourself. I'm going to get something to drink, you want something?"

"Yeah a coke would be nice." said Lynn as she made herself more comfortable.

Riva doesn't know what she's talking about, thought Lynn. Why would someone like Jesse like me when Riva and all the other girls are around? But It would be terrific if he did, she thought and smiled.

"Oh grow up," she said aloud.

"Were you talking to me?"

Startled, she looked up to find Jesse standing there.

"No, just to myself."

"Do you do that a lot? he asked, handing her a drink. "Riva said you wanted one."

"Thanks. And yes, I do talk to myself."

"That's OK; so do I."

Jesse sat down next to Lynn, and the two of them talked for a long time. Lynn felt comfortable with him. He listened to her, and she enjoyed hearing him talk. They told stories about their childhoods. They laughed together and came close to crying together when she talked about her mom. She told him how they would talk together for hours. Or how they would just sit quietly together.

Lynn tried to explain the emptiness she felt inside.

"Occasionally, someone will say something, or once in a while, something will happen, and I think I have to tell Mom," said Lynn. "Then I remember that she's gone. I want to talk to Dad about her, but he's always busy." she said, wiping away tears.

"You can always talk to me," said Jesse, taking her hand. He then gently pressed his lips to hers. Then he said good night. "Maybe Riva is right, maybe he does like me." she thought.

When Lynn got home, she ran up to her room, smiling. "Lynn did you have a nice time?" asked her dad.

"Yeah it was great."

That's good, see you in the morning, night."

Night Dad."

At least he'd asked this time, she thought to herself as she got into bed.

CHAPTER

3

"So how was the party?" asked Jade.

"It was OK," said Lynn.

"Well, tell me, was that guy there, what's his name?"

"Jesse, Yeah, he was there."

"So."

"It was just a party, nothing special."

"Oh, come on. What aren't you telling me? What'd you guys do, get loaded or something?" Jade said jokingly.

"Are you crazy? I don't do that. Why are you asking me something like that? I don't believe you." said Lynn, as she stormed off.

"Wait a minute," said Jade chasing after her. "What is with you? I was just joking, I know you don't do drugs."

"I'm sorry, I just …. let's talk about something else."

"OK, what about Jesse?"

"He's a nice guy, he's sweet, and he listens when you talk, he's funny, and I feel comfortable with him. Oh yeah, he's cute too." she said smiling. "I'm sorry for getting mad."

"Don't worry about it, it's no big deal. I'll pick you up at seven tomorrow morning. And Be ready, first day of school, I'd rather not be late."

"I'll be ready, see you then."

"Dad I'm home, Dad?" Lynn called as she went through the house.

She mounted the stairs to her room. She reached her door, just as the phone rang. It was her dad, calling to say he wouldn't be home till late.

Lynn shook her head as she hung up. She walked over to her desk, opened the middle drawer, and reached inside, pulling out a small wooden box. She opened it. There were three joints, a small ceramic pipe, rolling papers and a small bag of pot.

She took out a joint, closed the box, and

put it back in the drawer. She took some matches out of her purse and lit the joint. Taking a hit she lay back on her bed, smoking about half of it.

After a few minutes, Lynn began to giggle. Something seemed funny, although she couldn't remember what had made her laugh. She knew it had to be something amusing. She was so loaded that whatever she thought about made her laugh.

After a while, when she had calmed down, she got hungry. She went down to the kitchen and grabbed whatever she could find: Potato chips, cookies, a coke, cheese and crackers.

When she was finished eating, she went back upstairs to take a shower. Before she got to that, though, she started getting tired and depressed. Everything and everyone seemed so far off. She felt as though she was alone with no friends; that everyone had deserted her, especially her dad. She decided as tired as she was, the best thing to do was to just go to bed and hope things would be better by morning.

Lynn woke up the next morning to the sound of her alarm. The clock read 5:45 a.m. She turned on the radio and lay back in bed. There was a knock on her door.

"Lynn are you awake?" asked her dad, opening the door. "Good morning, are you ready to start your senior year?"

"Yeah, I guess so."

"You don't sound very excited."

"I am, I'm just waking up, that's all."

"Ok, I'll see you downstairs."

"Now that's weird," Lynn thought as she got dressed. "Dad hasn't checked on me like that in a long time."

She made her way down to the kitchen. To her surprise, her dad had made breakfast for them. They sat down together and ate pancakes. When they were finished, he offered to drive her to school. Surprised again, she told him Jade was picking her up. He said OK, wished her a good day, and left for work.

Lynn tried to understand what had just happened when she heard Jade at the door.

At school, Lynn concentrated on her classes. Lynn had always been excellent in school, had always gotten As and Bs, so she felt confident about her courses. She and Jade had History and Chemistry together, she, Riva, and Jesse had Crafts together, and the three of them had P.E. together. She ate lunch with Riva and Jesse, as Jade had a different lunch hour. After about two weeks, everyone was set in their classes and routines.

Lynn had never gotten loaded at school. One day, Riva brought some coke to school, and Lynn couldn't pass it up. The two of them went in the bathroom and stood in one of the stalls. Riva had a small vial with a tiny spoon attached, making it easier to use. Both of them snorted a couple of spoonfuls, then went out to meet Jesse on the lawn.

At first, Lynn was nervous, but she relaxed quickly. Jesse suggested that they go smoke a joint at the smoking circle. Lynn went with them but wasn't sure about smoking.

"Do you want a hit?", asked Jesse, handing her a joint. Lynn took a hit and she looked around.

"Don't worry." said Riva "The teachers never come over here."

They finished the joint just as the bell rang for Crafts. Then they went to class.

They were all working on separate projects, so they didn't have to worry about anyone paying too much attention to them.

"How ya doin'?" Riva asked Lynn

"I'm doin' great, how about you?"

"Just fine, but I think I'll go to the bathroom. Want to join me?" She said, patting her purse.

"Sure; you go first."

A few minutes later, Lynn joined Riva in one of the stalls. The two of them again snorted a couple of spoonfuls before going back to class.

From this point on, Lynn and Riva were always getting loaded at school.

"What was wrong with you today?" asked Jade.

"There was nothing wrong. Why?"

"You were acting strange."

"Thanks a lot, I'll return the compliment sometime."

"Well you were. You sat there and whistled while Ms Allen was trying to talk. Even after she asked you to stop. You've never done that before."

"So what? I wanted to whistle."

"Lynn, you were sent out of class. You know I think Riva has something to do with the way you've been acting."

"Hey, leave Riva out of this. She has nothing to do with it, she's not even in our class."

"Maybe not, but I don't like her. Ever since you met her you've been different.

"I think if you gave her a chance, you might like her."

"I doubt that,"

"Whatever. I gotta go. Jesse's coming over in a little while."

"You two have become some item. I really like him, I think the two of you make a cute couple."

"I'm glad you approve," said Lynn sarcastically. "I gotta go."

"OK, well, have fun tonight. See you tomorrow."

"Yeah, OK."

"I hope Riva and Jade start liking each other soon," said Lynn "because I'm getting real tired of hearing all this stuff from both of them. All they do is put each other down. And if it doesn't stop soon, one of them is going to be left behind."

"What are you talking about?" asked Jesse"

"I mean one of them will have to go."

"You mean you'd choose between them? That shouldn't be too hard. You and Jade have been friends too long to lose that." said Jesse.

"Yeah, but Riva and I have become really close; we like to party together. And you know Jade doesn't party."

"Getting loaded isn't all that important, is it? I think I would rather have a good friend than get loaded."

"I didn't say it was more important, but I enjoy it. You enjoy it too. We get loaded together. Besides, I thought you and Riva were friends. If it hadn't been for her, we might never have met." she said, putting her arms around him.

"And I'm glad about that," Said Jesse, holding her close. "But don't give Jade up before you think about it. Good friends like

Jade are hard to find."

"Ok," said Lynn, lightly caressed his cheek.

Jesse smiled and gently kissed her hand. He took her face in his hands and tenderly kissed her. With a fierce passion he hadn't shown before, he kissed her long and hard, leaving her breathless with an excitement she'd never experienced. She wanted more but was too scared, afraid of where it could go. With her hand on his chest, Lynn gently pushed him away. He brought her back to him and held her. Then he kissed her cheek and said goodnight.

CHAPTER

4

"**A**re you all right?" asked Jade.

"I'm fine." said Lynn.

"Are you sure?"

"I said I was fine. What are you doing here?

"I thought we would study together like we always do, but I didn't realize I had to have a reason to come over."

"I'm sorry, you don't."

"Well are we going to study?"

"No, I don't want to."

"Are you sure there's nothing wrong?"

"I'm fine, just because I don't want to study means something's wrong? Lighten up, will you? I've gotta make a phone call."

Lynn ran upstairs."I'll be down in a while," she yelled.

As she was dialing, she heard the door open and close and knew Jade had left. She was too interested in talking to Riva to be concerned about Jade. Lynn took out her last joint and smoked it while she waited to go meet Riva at Jake's.

As she reached the door to leave, her dad came in. "I'm glad you're here," he said. "I thought we could go out for a bite together."

I'm sorry, Dad, I already have plans."

"Can't you change them?"

"No, I'm going to study for a test with Jade, Its History, and she needs help."

"OK, maybe tomorrow. Just make sure you eat something. I know how the two of you get when you study together. You forget to eat."

"We will." Lynn said, smiling as she left.

Lynn and Riva didn't stay at Jake's long. Instead, they went over to a friend of Riva's. Lynn was a little anxious when they first walked in and saw people lying all over the floor. She watched as the smoke from a joint circle around someone's head. Others were snorting, and she was shocked to see a girl tie rubber tubing around her arm and then stick a needle in her inner elbow.

As they made their way to the back of the house, they passed rooms filled with people watching TV, sleeping, eating. Most of them looked like they hadn't had a bath in a month. And they didn't seem to care either.

When they reached the back of the house, Riva was greeted by a very good-looking blonde with blue eyes; he was neatly dressed. He didn't seem to fit in here. He offered Lynn a line of coke while he and Riva finished their business. She heard Riva call him Luke. Although they hadn't been introduced, he seemed to know her. He offered to take her home if she wanted to stay for a while. Lynn turned down the offer, telling him she already had plans with Jesse. They had become very close and spent as much time together as possible. Riva told Lynn she would make up an excuse to tell Jesse if she wanted to stay, But Lynn wasn't interested in staying.

When Lynn and Riva got to the car, Riva threw a big bag in the trunk and covered it with blankets. She got in on the drivers side, and Lynn hopped in on the passengers side.

"Are you nuts?" asked Riva

'What do you mean?"

Why didn't you stay with Luke? You would have had a great time."

"I told you, I'm meeting Jesse later. Besides, I didn't want to stay."

"So you turn down Luke for Jesse. Dumb move."

"What are you talking about? You know how I feel about Jesse. I don't want to see anyone else. Besides, I thought you were friends."

"We were, we are, but haven't you noticed that he's changed lately? He doesn't ever want to party anymore. He's become a real drag, you know."

"We still get loaded together sometimes.

But that doesn't matter. I still like him."

"Fine but if you change your mind let me know. I'm sure Luke will still be interested."

Lynn didn't say anything the rest of the way home. She just looked at Riva and wondered why she was pushing her towards Luke.

When Jesse arrived at Lynn's, she was loaded; She'd snorted a couple of lines of coke, and smoked a joint. Lynn asked Jesse if he wanted some, but he declined.

"I wish you hadn't gotten loaded before I came over," he said.

"Why not?"

"I just thought it would be nice to be together without being stoned for a change. I didn't think you had anymore."

"Well I didn't, but I went with Riva today to some guy's house to get some stuff. He was a pretty nice guy, he even gave me some pot to take with me. But I couldn't believe all the people who were there, and the things some of them were doing."

"What guy? What's his name?"

"Luke, why?"

"Luke!" said Jesse, raising his voice. "That bitch took you to Luke's place? He murmured to himself. "Well, that's the last time you go there."

"He said I could go over there whenever I wanted. Do you know him?"

"Oh yeah, I know him. He's bad news. Stay away from him."

"He didn't say anything when I mentioned your name."

"I'm not surprised. We didn't exactly part as friends."

"What do you mean?"

Jesse told her about how they'd met in the park when he was thirteen. He was just sitting alone, when this guy came up to him and started talking. They hit it off and started hanging out together.

Pretty soon, Luke had him smoking pot, as well as snorting coke and selling it.

One day when they were in the park, the cops showed up. Luke told Jesse to tell the police that the drugs were his because they wouldn't do anything to him because of his age. So, Jesse did.

And Luke was right: he got off. So, he kept selling for him. But Jesse got busted again and spent six months in juvenile hall. When he got out, Luke wanted nothing to do with him, saying the cops would be watching him; that getting caught twice, and going to juvie was not good for business. He told Jesse to get lost and not to come back.

"It doesn't sound like the Luke I met today, He probably just meant to stay away for a while in case they were watching you." said Lynn

"Yeah that's what he meant," said Jesse sarcastically. "I can't believe how naive you are sometimes, You don't know Luke at all. Just because he gave you a couple of lines doesn't mean he's OK. If anything, he probably wants something from you. He will make you pay next time. And I don't mean with money. I hope you understand."

"Yeah, I understand, just because you're on the outs with him you want me to be, too. Well, I like him and I'm going over to his place again with Riva when she goes."

"You do that, but why don't you do yourself a favor and think about it when you're not loaded. If you can remember what we talked about."

"Oh, that's cute. If you don't like me when I'm loaded, why don't you leave."

"That's a good idea, I think I will." said Jesse, turning to leave.

"That's a good idea, I don't want you here anyway, you're getting to be a real drag. You never want to smoke with me anymore, and you're always preaching about something. You don't want me to do anything anymore.

Well, I'll tell you, I'll do as I please, and you and nobody else is going to stop me."

"Oh, I'm sure of that. You're getting to be more like Riva every day."

"Thank you, I'll take that as a compliment."

"You would." said Jesse, shaking his head. "I can't believe how much you've changed. You're a different person. Jade said the same thing."

"You talked to Jade, so you two have been seeing each other? That's great, my boyfriend and my best friend."

"We haven't been seeing each other. We've talked a couple of times, she's worried about you, so I'm I."

"I'm fine, don't worry about me. So, did you tell her I smoke pot and snort coke?" Lynn asked, getting madder the more they talked. "I don't care if you did. Maybe she would loosen up a little if she smoked a joint once in a while. And I'm fine."

"That's why you're always stoned, cause you're fine. You're losing it Lynn. I'm afraid you're going to get hurt. And I didn't tell Jade; she already knew."

"I don't need your help, and I don't need you or Jade. So just get out. said Lynn, raising her voice.

"I'll leave but I'll be back."

"Don't bother." she said slamming the door.

"Where does he get off telling me I need help?" she thought. Riva was right; he has changed.

Lynn had a couple of lines of coke and then called Jade. She accused her of trying to steal Jesse, telling her they were not friends anymore and that she didn't want to see her again.

Jade tried her best to convince Lynn that she was not trying to steal Jesse, and that she would always be her friend. But Lynn wouldn't listen; she just hung up on Jade.

CHAPTER

5

Lynn had gotten into a routine of going over to Luke's house every day after school, if she went to school. Most of the time she would go straight to Luke's. At first, she went with Riva, then she started going by herself.

Except in class, she had not seen Jesse or Jade for quite a while. They had tried more than once to get a hold of her, but she wouldn't talk to them. She didn't want to talk to the two people she loved the most who had betrayed her.

And all this time, Riva was fanning the flames. She kept telling Lynn that she was better off with Luke. She also told her that she had seen Jade and Jesse together a lot, and that she saw them holding hands and kissing. The more Riva talked, the angrier and more confused Lynn got.

Luke was throwing a big party at his place. Lynn decided she was going to go and have the best time ever. She dressed in bell bottom jeans and a fringe blouse, with her hair hanging loose down her back. Lynn didn't know many of the people when she walked in. It was a completely different crowd than the people who were usually there.

She suddenly felt awkward and started thinking she should leave when she felt a hand on her shoulder.

Turning around, she thought it was Luke; instead, it was a dark-haired man, not bad looking, but something about him sent a shiver down her spine. Unexpectedly, he grabbed her and started kissing her. He was holding her so tightly that Lynn could hardly breathe.

When he finally let her go, Luke was standing next to them. Lynn was waiting for him to say something to the guy, but instead he just smiled and kissed her the same way.

When she started to protest, he quickly pulled her aside and told her not to make a big deal of it. And that she better stop acting as if she was something special. And start doing her part. Lynn was not sure what he meant, but she had a feeling she was going to find out.

The three of them went to the back room to do a few lines of coke. After a while, Lynn grabbed a drink and made her way back to the front room. They were passing joints around, so she sat down on the floor and took hits as they came around. She was more loaded than she'd ever been, feeling as if she were floating, yet it was hard for her to move. She was a little frightened, although she was also enjoying the feeling. Her thinking was blurred, and each time she would start to say something, she would stop in mid-sentence, trying to remember what she had been talking about.

After a while, Lynn heard loud noises and yelling from the back of the house. She wanted to know what was going on, so she got up and stumbled to the back.

When she reached the doorway and looked in the room, she felt like she was watching a movie in slow motion and not quite in focus. She shook her head, bent her head down, and closed one eye. It seemed to help her see clearer.

At first all she could see were two bodies

moving around. Then the faces became clear: it was Luke and Jesse. They were fighting, rolling on the floor and throwing punches at each other. Then another guy, one of Luke's friends, jumped in, grabbed Jesse, and held him while Luke beat him. All Lynn could see was Jesse covered in blood. She was paralyzed.

All of a sudden, she started to laugh. It had to be a joke, she thought, because Jesse would not be at one of Luke's parties; they hate each other. Luke stopped hitting Jesse when he heard Lynn. She came in, still laughing, and knelt down beside Jesse. She put her hand on his cheek and wiped the blood off. She stopped laughing when she realized it was real blood.

She turned to Luke. He just stood there staring at her, and something wasn't right. Lynn turned back and wiped the blood from Jesse's face, then realized it was actually Jesse. She was confused. Why was Jesse here, and why was Luke beating him up?

Lynn started crying as she tried to clean

Jesse up with her sleeve. Luke told his friends to take Jesse to his car. When she tried to help, Luke pulled her away. Looking up at him, she knew not to protest.

As Jesse was dragged out, everyone started laughing at him. Lynn stood there not knowing what to do, until Riva walked in. Riva would know what was happening.

She pulled Riva aside. "Jesse was here, they were hitting him," she cried. "Why was he here? Why were they hitting him?"

"Jesse wasn't here." laughed Riva.

"I saw him. Look blood."

"Man, you must really be out of it. What would Jesse be doing here? That was just a guy who tried to cheat Luke; he had it coming. Come on let's get you cleaned up."

"But I saw him, I wiped his face, it was Jesse, It was." cried Lynn putting her hands over her eyes.

Riva eyed Luke and nodded as she took

Lynn upstairs to the bathroom to clean her up. While she was wiping the blood away, Riva handed her the drink she had with her. "Here, drink this, you'll feel better."

Lynn drank it down. There was blood on her, but it couldn't have been Jesse's, she told herself. He wouldn't come to a party at Luke's. Maybe Riva was right.

When she was cleaned up, they went downstairs, to the back room, which had also been cleaned. Everyone was acting as if nothing had happened. They were drinking and passing joints around. All enjoying themselves. Lynn wasn't sure what had happened, So she decided to forget about it and enjoy herself.

After losing track of time, Lynn found herself back upstairs, this time in Luke's bed. Suddenly she felt chilled and realized she had nothing on. She was confused. How had she gotten there, and where were her clothes?

When she started to get up, a hand stopped her and pulled her back down. Startled, she turned to see the same dark-haired man who'd kissed her earlier. Lynn still did not know the man's name, or why he was with her now. He pulled her down again when she tried to get up. Her whole body was shaking with fright. He rolled on top of her, holding her down. He started kissing her as she struggled to get away. His hands started exploring her body, touching her in places he had no right to touch. The more she struggled, the harder he held her.

Lynn's mind was racing. Why was he doing this to her? Where was Luke? Why wasn't he helping her? She was screaming inside but nothing would come out. She was crying, but there were no tears.

After what seemed like an eternity, the man left, leaving Lynn hurt and confused. A few minutes later, Riva came in, smiling. "So, how was he?"

"How was he, do you know what he did?

"Yeah we all know what the two of you were doing," laughed Riva. "So tell me, was he as good as they say?"

Lynn wasn't sure what she was supposed to say. When Riva offered her a joint, she took a few hits. They did a line of coke while Lynn got dressed. By the time they finished another line, Lynn's mind was so foggy that she believed what Riva was telling her—-that it was a mutual thing between her and the dark-haired man. That she had gone after him. Lynn believed what she was told.

CHAPTER

6

Lynn woke up the next morning feeling as if she had been in a fight. She ached all over. As she sat up, she noticed a large bruise on her upper arm. She also found a bruise on her inner thigh.

She tried to remember how she had gotten those, and how she'd gotten home. But her mind was blank. She could not recall anything.

As she was getting out of bed, there was a knock on her bedroom door.

"Who is it?

"It's me." said Jade. She was enraged. "I need to talk to you. How could you let them do that to Jesse? You stood there and laughed. You've become a real piece of work, Lynn. As long as you have your drugs, to hell with everyone and everything. You're going to lose it if you haven't already."

"Lose what? And who did I let do what to Jesse?" Lynn asked, throwing her hands up.

"Yourself Lynn, yourself. And you know

who I'm talking about, and what they did."

"Look, if you're trying to tell me some-thing, just say it. And then you can get out."

"OK, I will. How could you let Luke and his friends beat Jesse up?"

"What are you talking about?" asked Lynn, shaking her head.

"Last night at Luke's party, that's what I'm talking about. You just stood there and laughed while they were beating him up. Then you watched as they dragged him out."

"You're nuts, why would Jesse be at Luke's party? They can't stand each other. And I don't remember anybody getting beat up, so if there's nothing else you want to say, leave."

"You really don't remember do you?" "What else happened that you can't remem-ber? Do you remember anything?"

"It's no big deal, but no. I don't"

"You can't remember anything and it's no

big deal. Oh Lynn, I'm scared for you," said Jade softly, I think you've already lost it." You need help before it's too late."

"All right, that's it, get out, quit trying to tell me what to do. You don't know anything about me anymore."

"I just want to help, you're still my best friend and I'm afraid for you. I don't want you to get hurt. So if you need anything, let me know." said Jade as she walked out of the room.

"Fine."

Lynn shut the door and sat with her head in her hands. Her head hurt. Could it be true about Jesse?

Lynn dialed his number, listening as the phone rang.

"Hello Mrs Taylor, this is Lynn, is Jesse there?"

"Yes he is, but he can't come to the phone right now. The doctor said he had to stay in bed for a while."

"The doctor? Does he have the flu or something?"

"Oh no, he's not sick. Jesse was beaten up last night. You didn't know?"

"Beaten up? Who did it?" asked Lynn with a shaky voice. "Will he be alright?"

"Well they're not sure who did it, and he won't say. He will be alright, but it will take a while. He has two cracked ribs and his face is bruised pretty badly. Why would anyone want to hurt Jesse? I don't understand."

"I don't know, I'm so sorry." was all Lynn could say as she hung up.

Lynn sat on the edge of the diving board as she took the last hit from the joint she was smoking. She stared into the water. The lights in the pool looked eerie, and the pool seemed to be calling her, inviting her in.

As she sat there, she could not get the thought of Jesse out of her mind. Had Luke beaten him up and had she been there, did she see it take place? Why couldn't she remember? Why would Jade say Luke did it when Jesse himself didn't even know? Or at least that's what he said.

Why would anyone want to hurt Jesse? He's so gentle and caring. What is going on? My best friend takes my boyfriend away, then says she didn't. Riva wants me with Luke. I just can't do this anymore.

Lynn stood up and dove into the pool. She swam back and forth several times, trying to block everything out.

She started getting tired, then got a cramp in her leg. She tried to work it out by rubbing it, but it seemed to cramp even more.

She tried to get to the edge of the pool, but her body was tired. No air, she couldn't get any air. Just water, water filling her lungs as she thrashed around trying to get her breath. Then, like nightfall, a thin veil of darkness covered her. It slowly got darker until there was nothing.

"She will be alright, won't she?" asked her dad.

"Yes, she'll be fine," said the doctor. You found her just in time. A few minutes more and it would have been too late."

As Lynn opened her eyes, she heard talking, then saw that one of the people talking was her dad.

"Lynn, Lynn can you hear me? asked her dad. It's Dad, well, hi there." he said with a smile as she opened her eyes. "How do you feel?"

"Tired and sore."

"That's probably from the paramedics giving you CPR. And you had a few bruises. You want to talk about them?" asked the doctor.

"What happened?" asked Lynn, ignoring the doctor.

"I was hoping you could tell me. Did you fall in? You had all your clothes on."

"I don't know, I can't remember much. I was sitting on the diving board and the next thing I'm in the hospital."

"That's OK, it will come back. But there is something else we need to talk about." said the doctor, turning to her dad.

"I jumped in," admitted Lynn.

"What?" asked her dad, surprised.

"I jumped in. I was swimming, then I got a cramp and couldn't get to the edge. I guess I panicked."

"Why were you swimming with your clothes on."

I don't know," she said, closing her eyes.

"Could it be that you didn't have control over what you were doing?"

"I don't know what you mean." said Lynn, turning her face away.

"Oh, I think you do, he said, taking her face in his hands. "Lynn, they found traces of marijuana and cocaine in your blood. And something called ecstasy. Lynn, why would you take that stuff? And why would you go swimming afterwards? Do you know how dangerous that is?

"That was the first time. I just wanted to know what it was like."

"The doctor said it was unlikely it was the first time."

"Well I did try some last night, but nothing happened, so I tried It again."

"We'll talk more about it tomorrow. The doctor wants to keep you overnight." He kissed her on the cheek, said goodnight and was gone.

Lynn was wondering why there would be ecstasy in her system. But she was too tired to really think about it. She turned over and went to sleep.

Lynn stared out the window of her room, down at the pool that almost took her life. She had no feelings about what had happened. To her, it was no big deal. It was just something that took place. I don't get it, she thought. Dad doesn't want me to go swimming by myself anymore. I didn't do anything to make him presume that something would happen again. At least he hadn't talked about the drugs they found in her system. She had convinced him it was the only times she had experimented with them.

Lynn shook her head and laughed as she lit a joint, thinking how easy it was to get out of trouble with her dad. He always believed her and never questioned anything she told him. But was it that he believed her or that he didn't care? Lynn wasn't sure, which brought tears to her eyes.

Jade and Jesse had tried to get in touch with Lynn after the pool incident, but she wanted nothing to do with them. She did see Riva, though. Riva brought her more pot and coke. Instead of cutting down after the accident she started doing even more.

She almost stopped going to school altogether. She would show up occasionally when she was bored just to see what was going on. She was called to the principal's office almost every time she showed up. Letters were sent to her dad, which she would destroy when they arrived. What she didn't know was that her dad had been in touch with the principle. They had talked several times.

"Lynn, come down here please." called her Dad.

"Yeah I'll be there in a minute." she answered

When she got downstairs, he said "Sit down, we have a few things to talk about."

"Yeah, like what? she challenged.

"Don't give me attitude. You haven't been going to school. And what's this about some guy named Luke beating up Jesse? Just because he wanted to talk to you at some party. And what kind of parties are you going to?

"Where did you hear that?"

"Jade told me. She called to talk to you, but you weren't here. I don't think you should be hanging around this guy Luke. He sounds like trouble."

"He's not, he's a nice guy. He likes me and I like him. Jade just wants to make trouble for me. She is mad that Riva and I are best friends. Which is her fault, since she stole Jesse from me. Don't believe anything she says, she lies all the time."

"Lynn that's enough. I don't want you seeing Luke anymore. And it might be a good idea if you didn't see Riva so much, either."

"Oh that's great; you take Jade's word over mine."

"Enough. Now about school. I talked to Mr. Bartlett. He told me you haven't been to school in weeks. He also said that he's sent letters to me, which I have not received."

"Well I haven't seen any letters." You know he doesn't really care about the students, he just sits in his office waiting for parents to come in."

"Oh Lynn, sighed her dad. "I'm going to be taking you to school for a while to make sure you go."

"You don't trust me anymore, is that it?"

"Lets just say I'm going to be checking on you a little more, that's all."

"Fine."

"Now you can go upstairs and do a little studying, and remember what I said about Riva and Luke. Lynn are you listening to me?"

"Yeah I heard you, but it's not fair."

"Maybe not, but that's the way it's going to be."

"Right."

CHAPTER

7

Lynn was a little surprised by what her dad had said. She hadn't expected that. It had been so long since he'd paid her any attention. She wasn't sure what to make of it. So, she decided to play it cool.

For the next couple of weeks, she did as her dad said to do. She went to school, studied, and stayed away from Riva and Luke. That is, until her supply ran out. Then she was back to ditching school, going to Luke's, and hanging out with Riva.

Things changed at Luke's. He acted differently and started making demands on her. She had to start selling, or he would cut her off.

So, she started selling to the kids at school. She was getting in deeper with Luke, and, at the same time, getting herself deeper into drugs. That was not all he wanted; he also told her she had to start sleeping with him, or she could get out.

So without any feelings, she slept with Luke. She was so loaded most of the time she didn't even know what was going on. When she was coherent, she was numb. Lynn had learned to close herself off from her feelings. And before she knew it, she was being passed around from one guy to the next. More and more, Luke was ignoring her and spending time with a new girl that Riva had brought to him. He had no more time for her.

"Luke, what's going on?" asked Lynn. "I came over to get some stuff, and your friend over there said I'm cut off. What does that mean?"

"Just that you're cut off, there is no more for you."

"Why? I've got money, I've done everything you told me to. I've been selling and I've even slept with guys you told me too."

"Yeah well look at yourself, you're a slob, your hair looks like it hasn't been washed or combed in weeks. Your clothes are always messy looking."

"I promise to clean myself up," said Lynn as she swept her hair back and tried to straighten her clothes. "I'll wash my hair, I'll get new clothes. I promise. So, how about some coke and a lid of your best smoke."

"Sorry, Lynn, you're too much of a risk. You don't even know what you're doing half the time. I can't take the chance anymore. You're just going to have to get someone else to supply you. Look, I've gotta go. I've got people waiting for me. Time for you to leave, and don't come back.

"But I don't know where to go! cried Lynn.

He showed her to the door.

Lynn was stunned. She couldn't believe Luke would do that to her. She didn't know what to do.

She thought of Riva. Riva would know where to go. Lynn was starting to panic. What if Riva wasn't home? Or if she didn't know anyone else? What then?

She remembered Riva talking about someone downtown. Lynn had thought he didn't sound like someone she would want to go to. But right now, she didn't care what kind of person he was.

When she got to Riva's, Riva was not happy to see her.

"What the hell are you doing here? Look at you. I told you if you were to come over, you better look halfway decent. You're a mess."

"I only came over to find out where that guy lives, the one you told me about, the one in town. Luke cut me off."

"And you're surprised? Lynn go home, clean up, and I'm sure Luke will give you what you want."

"No, he won't, he said no more at all. That's why I need you to take me to that guy."

"Just a minute," said Riva as she went inside, leaving Lynn on the porch. "Here take this, it's all I have." But Lynn wasn't satisfied.

"That's not what I want. I don't have anything left. A couple of joints aren't going to last. I've got money, see?" said Lynn, holding out her hand.

"Lynn, that's never been a problem. Where did you get it this time?"

"I sold a pair of earrings that Dad gave me. Now are you going to take me to that guy's place."

"I'll tell you where he lives, but you'll have to go by yourself."

"Fine, now how do I get there?"

Lynn made her way downtown, walking, to where Riva said to go. She had never been in that part of town. As she walked, she had the feeling she'd better go back, but the urge for drugs was stronger.

When she got to the address, the building looked like it was about to fall down. As she walked in, the smell made her sick. The odor was strong, and as she looked around, she saw why. There was trash all over the floor and water running down the hall like a small stream. She made it to the stairs, stood there a minute, and went up.

The second floor didn't look any better. As she climbed the stairs, she heard voices. When she reached the top, things got quiet again. She slowly walked down the hall, through piles of trash, to the room number Riva had given her.

When she knocked, a voice from behind the door answered, then, suddenly, the door swung open. There stood a man with long stringing hair, in dirty clothes.

"Riva sent me," said Lynn, shaking with fear.

He motioned for her to come in. He didn't say a word, just closed the door behind her and walked to the next room.

Walking through the room, she looked around. It looked the same as the hall. Trash everywhere, paint peeling off the walls, and the same strong odor.

When she'd crossed the room, she stood in the doorway looking in. The room was empty except for a table where the man sat who had opened the door. And there was a mattress. A man and woman were sitting on it, smoking from a small pipe.

As Lynn reached the table, she was startled by a shriek. The woman on the mattress was pulling at her hair and scratching at her body as if there were something crawling on her. The woman leapt up and ran to the open window, and, without hesitation, jumped.

Lynn was terrified; she couldn't believe what had just happened. She slowly walked to the window, where the long-hair man was standing. Looking down, she saw the woman lying on the pavement motionless, her body distorted. The two men ran into the hall, and by the time Lynn had made it to the door, they were gone.

In a daze, she made her way downstairs. Outside, a small crowd had gathered around the woman's body. Lynn turned and started walking away.

She walked for miles, not knowing where

she was going, until she looked up. She found herself in front of Jade's house. She stood there, looking up at Jade's room.

Lynn started to walk away when she heard Jade calling her name. She stopped and turned around. Jade stopped before she got to Lynn, surprised by what she saw: she was pale, her eyes were fixed and glassy, her hair and clothes were a mess.

Jade took a couple of steps toward her, but before she could reach her, Lynn passed out. Jade called to her mom, and with the help of her parents, they got Lynn upstairs to Jade's room. As Jade was washing Lynn's face, her mom called Lynn's dad.

When Lynn came to, she sat up and put her arms around Jade's neck. She started crying uncontrollably. Jade held her until she fell back on the bed in a heap.

CHAPTER

Lynn was resting when her dad came into the room. As he sat down next to her, he gathered her into his arms. She felt so small. She held him and felt safer than she had felt in a long time.

Her dad asked where she had been all these weeks. Through tears, she told him about the places she'd been staying. The nights she spent outside. And then she told him about the woman who jumped out the window when she had gone to the apartment to get drugs.

Lynn promised that she was done: no more drugs. Her dad told her she would have to go through a program, that she needed help. He also called 911 to tell them the story she'd told him. The cops showed up at Jade's to take Lynn's statement.

Lynn was doing well. She was happy for the first time in months. She was going to counseling, and she'd gotten a job at Jake's. Her relationship with her dad had become strong again. She and Jade had grown close again, and Jesse was back in her life. Luke and Riva were out of her life.

Then one day when she was at work, Riva walked in.

"So this is where you've been hiding yourself."

"Do you want something?" asked Lynn.

"Yeah how about a hit to start with. Said Riva grinning.

"Look, I'm working. Do you want to order or not?"

"I'll have a coke. And how about you, wouldn't you like some coke?

"No thanks, I quit."

"Yeah right, Luke's been asking about you. He would like to see you. Why don't you come with me? I'm on my way over to his place now."

"I can't, I'm working."

"Well when do you get off?"

"In about an hour."

"Great I'll come back and get you."

"I can't. I already have plans."

"See ya later," said Riva, ignoring her.

Lynn was determined not to go with Riva. She did not want that anymore. Besides, she had plans with Jade. But when Riva came back, she left with her. "What harm would it do to see Luke again?" She thought.

When they got to Luke's, he hugged her and told her how happy he was to see her, and how much he'd missed her. While they sat talking, Riva lit up a joint, Luke took a couple of hits, then passed it to Lynn.

At first, she refused, then reached out and took it.

Luke welcomed her back. "So why don't you come by tonight and party with us?" he asked.

"I can't, I'm busy."

"Come on, you can get out of whatever it is, can't you? asked Riva. We're going to do some heavy partying."

"She's right, it's going to be one helluva party."

"No, I don't think so this time," said Lynn, as she snorted lines Riva had set up.

"Ok but you're missing out." said Luke.

"Maybe next time." said Lynn, getting up to leave. "Thanks."

Lynn had made up her mind to not go to the party. She and Jade had plans that she was going to keep.

When she showed up at Jade's. Jade was furious. "I can't believe it, you're loaded. What's with you? Don't you remember what happened to that girl. You promised you were finished with drugs. You were doing so well. What happened?

"Nothing happened, Riva came to see me at work and I went back to Luke's with her, that's all. It's no big deal."

"No big deal. That doesn't sound like you when you're straight, only when you're loaded."

"Get off my back. So I got loaded, so what."

"I think you should come in and I'll call your dad for you. He can come pick you up."

"Forget it, I'm not going home. In fact, I think I'll go to Luke's party, cause you're a drag. And I'm feeling too good to let you bring me down."

"Wait a minute." said Jade grabbing her arm. "I'm not going to let you go anywhere in your condition."

"You can't stop me," Lynn said, pulling away. "Why don't you wake up? Everybody gets loaded. But since you don't, you can keep your preaching to yourself."

She turned and headed toward her car, Jade right behind her.

"Well if you're going, so am I." declared Jade, as she got in the car.

"Get out of my car, you're not going with me."

"Oh yes I am."

"Fine, but you're not going to like it."

Lynn took off down the street, running stop signs, lights. Barely slowing down to go around corners. Jade tried to get her to slow down, but the more she tried, the faster Lynn went.

When they came to a corner, Lynn stepped on the gas. She just missed hitting another car and went out of control. The car swerved, flipped, rolled and landed upside down.

Opening her eyes Lynn saw blood running down Jade's face. She tried reaching for her but the pain was too much. She passed out.

When she woke up, Lynn found herself

in the hospital. Her head throbbed, and she had a cast on her arm. She was sore all over. The extent of her injuries were a broken arm and a few stitches on her forehead.

She tried to find out about Jade, but none of the nurses would tell her anything.

When her dad came in, she asked about Jade. He said nothing, the doctor wouldn't tell her anything either. But he did start asking her questions, like how much she smoked and how much coke she'd had.

She tried to talk her way out of it, but it was no use. They knew.

Lynn looked at her dad, who looked old and tired. There was sadness in his eyes. And she knew it was because of her. She had broken her promise to him.

Lynn tried to say she was sorry, but he just looked at her, and she knew something terrible had happened.

The next time she asked about Jade, he told her. She was hurt badly, with three broken ribs, a punctured lung, and a head injury.

She was in a coma. They didn't know if she was going to make it or not. Lynn couldn't believe it. She was in shock. Her best friend could die because of her actions. Because she couldn't turn down a chance to get loaded even after her promise to everyone.

When Lynn walked in to Jade's room, she began to cry. Jade was hooked up to all kinds of equipment.

Lynn sat down next to Jade and took her friend's hand.

"I'm so sorry, I wouldn't hurt you on purpose for anything. But that is what I did, I hurt you more than anyone else ever has. Please forgive me, please don't die. I love you. Please just come back to us."

Lynn came back and sat holding Jade's hand for days, but there was no change. She was not getting any better.

She did a lot of praying, asking for forgiveness, asking for Jade's life. She stayed with Jade until they would kick her out. Then she would go back a few minutes later. She talked to her about their friendship, all the things they have done, and the things they would do together in the future.

One day when Lynn was talking about something they'd done together, Jade had opened her eyes. Lynn jumped up to get a nurse, but Jade still had a hold of her hand and would not let go.

Lynn sat back down and started crying. She put her head down on the bed next to Jade and asked for forgiveness. Jade lay her hand on Lynn's head. Lynn cried harder, knowing she was forgiven, but could she forgive herself?

The nurses came in and took all the equipment out of Jade's room. They told Lynn that Jade would be OK, but she still had a long way to go. With almost killing Jade she realized she had a problem.

Lynn now knew that she had an addiction. She knew that with her dad's help, and going back to therapy, she could beat it this time.

ACKNOWLEDGMENTS

I would like to thank Catherine Dee for her excellent editing of my book.

I would especially like to thank Asya Blue for her vision that matched my own for the cover. And for her exceptional work on the interior design.

www.ingramcontent.com/pod-product-compliance
Lightning Source LLC
Chambersburg PA
CBHW071540100726
47908CB00004B/1449